Tooth Fairy

Peppa and George are eating
their favourite food, spaghetti!
"Slurp! Sloooop!"

Suddenly something falls
onto Peppa's plate.
"What's that?" cries Peppa.
"It's your tooth!" laughs Daddy Pig.

"If you put the tooth under your pillow tonight the Tooth Fairy will pay you a visit. She will take the tooth and leave you a shiny coin!" says Mummy Pig.

"Goodnight Peppa! Goodnight George!" says Mummy Pig. "Goodnight my little piggies!" grunts Daddy Pig.

Peppa puts her tooth under
the pillow for the Tooth Fairy.
"Let's stay awake all night and
see the Tooth Fairy," says Peppa.
"Snort!" George giggles.

"George, where's the Tooth Fairy?" Peppa asks. "She's very late!" But George is so tired he has fallen fast asleep.

"I'm not going to go to sleep . . .
I'm . . . zzz, zzz," snores Peppa.
When everything is quiet,
something appears at the window.

The Tooth Fairy has arrived . . .
But Peppa is fast asleep.
The fairy pushes a shiny coin under
the pillow and takes Peppa's tiny tooth.

"Peppa, George, wake up! It's morning,"
says Mummy Pig brightly.
"Did the Tooth Fairy come?"
Daddy Pig asks.
"No," says Peppa sadly.

"Let's look under your pillow,"
says Daddy Pig. "Look Peppa!
The Tooth Fairy has been and
she's left you a coin!"

"Hooray! Hee! Hee! Hee!"
Peppa laughs. "Grunt! Next time
I will stay awake and I will see
the Tooth Fairy! Hee! Hee!"